This book belongs to:

_____

Digital art by Callaway Animation Studios under the direction of David Kirk in collaboration with Nelvana Limited.

This book is based on the TV episode "Giddy Up Bugs," written by Michael Stokes, from the animated TV series
Miss Spider's Sunny Patch Friends on Nick Jr., a Nelvana Limited/Absolute Pictures Limited co-production in
association with Callaway Arts & Entertainment, based on the Miss Spider books by David Kirk.

Nicholas Callaway, President and Publisher
Cathy Ferrara, Managing Editor and Production Director
Toshiya Masuda, Art Director • Nelson Gómez, Director of Digital Technology
Joya Rajadhyaksha, Associate Editor • Amy Cloud, Associate Editor
Raphael Shea, Senior Designer • Krupa Jhaveri, Designer
Bill Burg, Digital Artist • Christina Pagano, Digital Artist • Dominique Genereux, Digital Artist

Special thanks to the Nelvana staff, including Doug Murphy, Scott Dyer, Tracy Ewing, Pam Lehn,
Tonya Lindo, Mark Picard, Jane Sobol, Luis Lopez, Eric Pentz, and Georgina Robinson.

Library of Congress Cataloging-in-Publication Data available upon request.

Distributed in the United States by Viking Children's Books.

Visit Callaway Arts & Entertainment at www.callaway.com.

ISBN 978-0-448-44505-2

10 9 8 7 6 5 4 3 2 1   07 08 09 10

First edition, January 2007

Printed in China

Giddy Up Bugs

David Kirk

CALLAWAY

NEW YORK

2007

Sawyer explained that cowbugs watch over aphids as they suck the sap out of plants. In the aphids' bodies, the sap turns into sweet honeydew, which ants harvest.

"Did we hear someone mention honeydew?" called Ned and Ted.

The new cowbugs followed with a cry as the aphids set off to feed.

Sawyer asked the ant brothers to help, too.

"Oooh, we'd love to . . . if we didn't have to rest," Ned said.

"We're weak," Ted added, "weak from hunger."

One fine day, a wagon pulled by four aphids came thundering into Sunny Patch, startling Squirt, Shimmer, and Bounce. Steering the wagon was Sawyer the ant.

"Howdy, partners!" Sawyer cried, sweeping off her big hat.

The cowbugs had come to camp out at the meadow for the honeydew harvest. Bounce, Squirt, and Shimmer offered to lend a hand.

"You're already genuine cowbugs, then!" Sawyer exclaimed. "Rule number one on the frontier is: cowbugs always help each other out."

Sawyer taught the new cowbugs to track the aphids by looking for footprints and trampled grass. Curled-up leaves would show what plants they had visited.

"Now, let's hit the trail and harvest some honeydew!" Sawyer hollered. "And remember rule number two: a cowbug is never lazy."

After a long day of hard work, it was time for a scrumptious honeydew supper.

Sawyer told Ned and Ted they could only eat if they helped out. "Cowbug code," she said firmly.

Mumbling and grumbling, the two ants started cooking.

That night, while the aphids slept all alone in their pen, Ned and Ted realized there might be an easier way to get honeydew.

"Neddy-boy," said Ted, "we may just have to borrow those aphids for a while."

The next morning, Sawyer organized a rodeo for her newest cowbugs.

Sawyer grinned as she told them rule number three: "A cowbug knows how to have fun."

"Yee-haw!" Squirt cried as he bounced up and down on a branch. "I'm bronco branch-busting!"

When they returned to the camp, the cowbugs couldn't believe their eyes. The aphids were gone!

"The aphids have been bug-napped!" Sawyer gasped.

"Don't worry," Shimmer assured her, "we'll help you track them!"

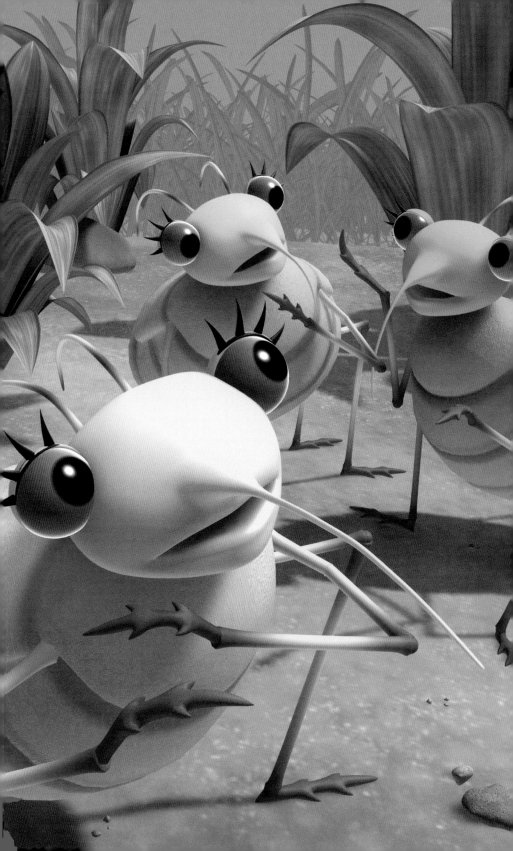

Meanwhile, Ned and Ted could not agree on how to herd their "borrowed" aphids.

"Yee-hoot!" shouted Ned.

"No, it's 'Yaw-hee'!" insisted Ted.

"Let's ditch these dippy dudes," murmured one of the aphids.

They all snuck off while Ned and Ted were fighting.

Sawyer really started to worry about the missing aphids when a windstorm began to blow.

The cowbugs followed the aphids' tracks and found Ned and Ted. The ant brothers began to shake and confessed everything.

"We didn't mean any harm!" they said, pointing in the direction where they'd left the aphids.

Shimmer spotted a plant with curled-up leaves. The aphids were near.

"Hooray!" she shouted. "I found them!"

But just then, a big
tumbleweed blew through,
trapping one of the aphids and
blowing him toward a scary
slither-snake.

"Quick!" said Sawyer.
"Wrangle me down that
bucking branch!"

quirt, Shimmer, and Bounce tossed Sawyer into the air. She landed in front of the tumbleweed and rescued the aphid . . . just before the snake chomped down.

Back at the camp, Ned and Ted
scrubbed dirty dishes as Sawyer
hitched the aphids to their wagon.

"Thanks for all your help,
everybuggy," cried Sawyer as
she led the aphids into the sunset.
"Yee-haw, and giddy-up bugs!"

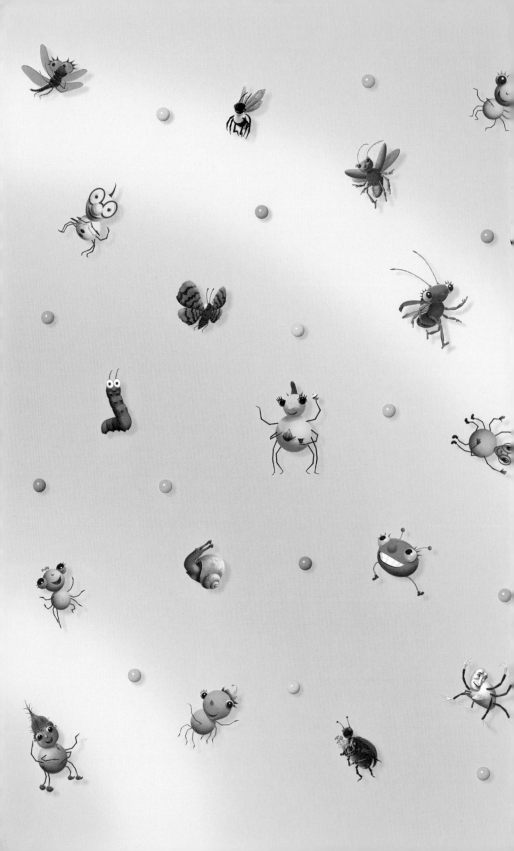